CAN YOU SEE IT?

VICTOR PAUL

Copyright © 2021 by Victor Paul

Follow Victor Paul on Instagram: instagram.com/victorpauldomain

First paperback edition July 2021

Book Design by Daniela Owergoor
Typeset by Post Pre-press Group

A catalogue record for this book is available from the National Library of Australia

ISBN 978-0-6450135-6-6 (paperback)
ISBN 978-0-6450135-7-3 (ebook)

PROLOGUE

Western Australia, 2016

Evil was about to erupt in the old prison. The painting needed just one finishing touch. Working through the ghostly hours in an execution chamber would certainly not appeal to any regular artist, but Antonio Rossi was no conventional artist. His abstract art pieces often drew the attention of the public, who wondered how and where he got his inspiration. He had kept it all a secret throughout his career. He revelled in his art being mysterious to everyone. Needless to say, this artwork's inspiration was certainly going to be a secret. Moreover, he couldn't risk his best friend of many years, Mario, getting fired for letting him in.

Under normal circumstances, no person would be allowed in this prison past midnight, let alone allowed to freely wander the execution chamber in the dead of the night. In fact, the prison would be closed to the general public once the night tours were completed. The tour guide would ensure every person left the prison and the guard would secure the gates, preventing anyone from entering. Tonight, Antonio had asked Mario, who was on duty, to sneak him in.

The prison, which first opened in 1855, used to hold England's most notorious criminals in an effort to relieve overcrowded English prisons. By the late 1860s, the transportation of British criminals ceased, and only local convicts were sent to that prison. By the early 1990s, the prison was closed down due to its deteriorating conditions. The history of the prison remained in its walls long after it had been shut down. Rather than tear down the prison, the local government turned it into a prison museum. The prison had a day and night tour enabling the public to view the prison and learn of its history.

Antonio had participated in one of the prison's night tours. He knew the stories; the terrible things that had taken place in the once notorious prison. It was on this tour that Antonio found one particular room that resonated with him; the execution chamber. Mario had mentioned to him after the tour that on a certain date every year, the prison authorities ensured the execution chamber was out of bounds to everyone. This intrigued Antonio even further. He came to know that an extremely evil convict known as the Beast Man was executed on that date and that the executioner committed suicide the same day he executed the Beast Man.

Mario shared with Antonio that strange things seemed to happen to anyone who went into the execution chamber on the date that the Beast Man was executed. Mario went on to reveal to Antonio that there were several inexplicable deaths and suicides associated with the chamber on that particular date. The prison committee decided that the execution chamber was strictly out of bounds to anyone on that day each year. This information drew Antonio all the more to paint in the infamous chamber. He wanted to bring out the darkness of the execution chamber where this notorious figure was put to death.

Antonio had gone almost twelve months without painting, and the execution chamber had finally inspired him to paint something. The prison authorities, however, had not granted him his request to work in the chamber. So, Antonio found a way around it.

Antonio convinced Mario that no one other than them would know about it. He would simply need a few hours to complete his painting. He would be in and out of the prison before the next guard arrived to start his shift. It wasn't without hard-earned convincing that Antonio managed to get Mario to agree to his idea. Nothing seemed to deter Antonio.

Now Antonio was about to complete his masterpiece. His final stroke of paint found itself in the middle of the canvas, surrounded by several other circular strokes of black and grey. He withdrew his brush and examined his work, satisfied with what he saw. A quick glance at the watch on his white-haired wrist showed that it was three in the morning. He was supposed to give Mario a call, as discussed, to come get him once he was done. His t-shirt was soaked in sweat, a result of the airless, still room to which he had been confined for the last few hours.

His eyes fixated on the centre of the canvas for a moment. Suddenly, he felt a presence. From midnight till now, he had not heard any sound other than his own breathing. Now he heard murmurs throughout the old prison's execution chamber. He wondered if it could be Mario just outside the execution chamber door. He strained his ears. This wasn't the sound of a human being. It sounded like the roar of a beast. The hair on the back of his neck stood up.

The murmurs got louder and louder. He heard a creaking sound behind him. He turned around and saw the gallows' noose swaying from side to side. His eyes widened. A sharp shiver crept down his spine. He felt a chilling touch on his shoulder and turned around swiftly. The muffled murmurings stopped. The noose stopped swaying. An overpoweringly foul smell flooded the room. Antonio hurriedly packed up his brushes. He wanted to get out of the room, that instant. His heart was pumping so loudly that his ears were filled with the sound of its frantic beats.

Antonio reached into his pocket for his mobile phone. He frantically dialled for Mario to come to the execution chamber at once. He wished at that moment he had listened to his dear friend's advice. His teeth chattered violently as he waited for the phone to ring.

His phone's battery died just as Mario answered. He decided to leave the chamber without any further delay. His heart didn't have the strength to stay in that chamber alone, not even for another minute. He decided to drop all his things, leave the painted canvas behind and head for the door.

And then Antonio saw it. He tried to scream, but nothing came out of his mouth. The sharp claws of the Beast Man swiped across his face. He collapsed to the ground. His heart skipped a beat and then it stopped completely.

CHAPTER 1

Western Australia, 2017

Jack had finally made it to the closing-down art gallery sale. Though fairly new to the business, Jack had been successful enough to start his own gallery. So far, the day had kept him busy. He used his lunch break to quickly nick off to see if he could find himself a deal. He left the gallery in the capable hands of his art intern, Casey, sensing that there might be interesting pieces that he could purchase.

An old man sat behind the store counter watching the cars go by with little interest, as Jack crossed the street to the closing-down sale. Jack's impression of the old man was that he looked weary, as though life had beaten him to the ground. The old man's shoulders drooped down sadly. In front of the counter was one last painting waiting to be sold.

Jack looked at the sign in bold that hung in front of the store's clear glass window: *Closing-down: everything must go.* He pushed the door open; the old man's eyes came alive when he saw him. Jack's eyes immediately fell upon a gloomy-looking painting that reflected the old man's state. The painting was dull, yet it would capture the attention of anyone who looked at it. Jack stood face to face with the old man, studying the full moustache and beard that matched the man's white hair.

'You're just in time. I was about to close up and get myself a cold beer. This heat is unbearable.'

'I know. It's a hot afternoon. Is that the only piece you've got left?'

'Yes, it is. Antonio Rossi's final work.'

'The famous Antonio Rossi who passed away recently?'

'That's correct. Do you want to buy it?'

Jack sensed a kind of urgency in the old man's voice. Jack didn't know if he was in a rush to close the store for the day or simply wanted to sell the very last painting so that the sale would be over and done with. He knew, being the owner of a gallery himself, that you should never rush the sale of any artwork. Even if it was closing time, he wouldn't place any urgency in his tone when speaking with a potential buyer. That was not the way art was sold—at least not from his point of view.

He looked at the price tag and cupped his chin with his hand. The painting was covered in circular strokes of blacks and greys, all leading to an eerie centre. Jack looked closer. In the centre of the painting, there seemed to be a white blurry image of something. He couldn't quite determine what it resembled.

'Do you want it or not? I can give you a better price,' said the old man, managing to break Jack's intense observation.

'Ten thousand is way off my budget for a single piece, but—' said Jack as he looked at the hefty price tag.

A loud car whizzed past the store, drowning out Jack's voice mid-sentence.

'Six hundred and sixty-six dollars is fine with me. Sold!' exclaimed the old man.

'You are selling it to me for six hundred and sixty-six dollars?'

'I maybe old, but I'm not deaf. You've got yourself a deal, son.'

Jack stood there, confused, as the old man punched the numbers into the point-of-sale machine that awaited payment. Jack looked at the painting once again, unable to comprehend what had just happened. He hesitated, wondering if the old man was being serious.

'Are you going to pay for it or what? I want to close the store. I'm done with it.'

'Yeah, I'll pay for it. It's six hundred and sixty-six dollars, right?'

'That's what we agreed on.'

The sale numbers presented themselves across the machine. As Jack stood at the counter ready to pay, he noticed a large stack of overdue bills. An eviction letter caught his eye. Jack swiped his Mastercard, thoughts racing through his head. He wondered what had happened to this old man for him to lose his gallery.

Jack watched as the old man hurriedly wrapped the painting with brown paper and handed it over to him.

'It's all yours now,' he said, decidedly.

Jack left the store, puzzled as to what had just taken place. It all seemed to have occurred in a matter of seconds. He paused for a moment across the street and gazed at the gallery. He couldn't help but feel curious about how quickly the old man closed up the store and locked it behind him. The old man stood still, looking briefly into his store. Then he shook his head, as if in disappointment, and walked away.

The whole transaction had been strange; he still couldn't come to terms with how the old man had sold him a piece for a price that he didn't even offer. *Was the old man mistaken?* he wondered. He unlocked his car and placed the wrapped-up artwork on the passengers' seat. On the brown wrapping paper appeared to be four tear lines—as if a claw had torn through it. Confused, he quickly checked to see if the painting had been accidentally damaged. *He heaved a sigh of relief.* Maybe the paper was already torn, he thought to himself.

As he drove off from the parking lot to his own art gallery, he pondered the whole incident that had just taken place. He did, however, find himself happy with the deal he had managed to get. Despite the unsettling nature of the sale itself, he was now in possession of Antonio Rossi's last ever masterpiece.

CHAPTER 2

Jack carefully placed the painting in a prominent area of his art gallery where it would catch the eye of anyone who opened the door. Jack was excited to tell anyone and everyone about the latest addition to his collection.

'That's a great spot for that piece. You still haven't told me how much you bought it for,' said Casey.

'It's a secret,' said Jack with a mysterious smile.

'Oh come on. I've worked for you for over a year now. You can tell me ...'

'Some things are better left a secret, Casey.'

'Alright then ... How much should I price it for—or is that a secret as well?' laughed Casey.

'Price it at ten thousand,' said Jack, looking at the painting confidently.

Jack had been trying to get his hands on such a

masterpiece for quite some time. He'd run his gallery with tireless effort and his hard work was written all over its walls. Until now, it had been a relatively small operation. Needless to say, owning a genuine Rossi masterpiece made him jubilant.

Jack was eager to uncover the essence of the painting. He looked at it closely. *What message was Rossi trying to convey? Why the black and grey, and the white figure in the middle? Where did he get his inspiration from?*

'God ... You scared me Casey,' said Jack as he felt Casey touch his arm.

'Aren't you going to answer your phone? It's been ringing non-stop,' said Casey as she looked at him with concern.

'Sorry ... Yeah, thanks.'

Jack reached into his pocket for his mobile phone.

'Hey, I won't be free to drop by in the afternoon to see the painting. I'll come over once you're about to close up. Is that okay?' said Amanda.

'Yeah, that's fine. I'll see you later then, love.'

He caught sight of Casey looking over at him, concerned.

'I got lost in deep thought, that's all,' he said, waving his hand dismissively.

'Okay, just don't get so lost that you can't hear your own phone ring,' said Casey.

The longer Jack looked at the painting, the more he became drawn to it. He told himself that he would soon uncover the mystery behind it.

CHAPTER 3

Jack couldn't wait to show Amanda this prized painting. He had closed for the day and was eagerly awaiting her arrival. Whilst waiting, he found himself once more taking a closer look at the artwork's finer details. He took a step back and admired the piece. *A bit dark for me, but I'm sure Rossi was trying to convey something important*, he muttered.

Side-tracked, he began thinking about what Amanda would have to say about the prominent painter's work. Jack had shared every moment of happiness with Amanda, from the time he managed to start his own gallery, to the very first art piece he purchased; he cherished every moment with her. As he sat back on his chair and waited, he momentarily thought of Amanda and all the good times he had had with her. After two years of seeing each other, he had managed to convince her to move in with him into his cosy house. He remembered joking with her that the house had too much space for just him and his dog Rusty. She liked Jack's sense of humour. He had an ambitious character that she often said she found very attractive. Jack couldn't wait to break the news that a renowned painter's artwork now sat proudly in his gallery.

He wasn't too sure what Amanda would think of the painting itself. One thing Jack knew about Amanda for sure was that she wasn't a fan of dull colours. She dressed colourfully herself. She often gave Jack insight into what she liked around his gallery. He went back to analysing the painting. It had all the hallmarks of being painted by an expert, yet it delivered a very bleak message of some kind. The painting was somewhat eerie. To Jack, the ghostly mark in the middle seemed particularly mysterious.

He placed his hand on his chin and wondered why he had even bought the painting to start with. It certainly wasn't something he would have usually picked. However, it was Rossi's final piece, and it had sold at the incredibly low price of six-hundred-and-something dollars. As an art dealer, he knew the piece was worth much more. He also knew the old man had been desperate to sell it and certainly hadn't pushed for a higher price. He smiled to himself as he thought about how lucky he had been—right place, right time.

He glanced at the window of his shop and saw Amanda smiling and waving to him from across the street. He quickly grabbed a large cloth and covered the artwork.

'I've got a surprise to show you,' said Jack as Amanda entered the gallery.

'Well, you have been talking about this purchase more than any other, so let's see it.'

'Voila! This is the last painting of the late Antonio Rossi,' said Jack as he uncovered the painting.

Amanda's smile dropped and she cocked her head to the left. He certainly hadn't expected that reaction. He waited for her to say something. The seconds of silence were making him impatient for her opinion. He waited a few seconds more and then the realisation struck him.

'It's the colours isn't it? Not colourful enough?'

'No ... It isn't the colours. It's just ...'

'Just ...?' prompted Jack.

'Just a strange painting, don't you think?'

Jack knew she was right. He felt that the art piece was strange; he just wanted Amanda to reaffirm that despite the darkness, strangeness and lack of colour, she could see that it was indeed a masterpiece.

'Well, you can say that, but hey—you won't believe how much I paid for it.'

'Oh no Jack, don't tell me you used up all your savings just to buy this piece?'

'You're not going to believe it. It was just over six hundred dollars.'

'You sure know how to get a good bargain, don't you? How did you manage to do that?' she said with a big smile.

'Well, let's just say I was in the right place at the right time.'

Later, Jack closed the gallery and locked the door, leaving hand in hand with Amanda and feeling a great sense of pride and excitement.

CHAPTER 4

Jack looked at all the artworks in his gallery; not one item had moved the entire week since he'd purchased Rossi's painting. The new addition hadn't quite appealed as much as he'd hoped it would. No one was really interested in anything more than a browse through his shop. Jack couldn't understand the sudden drop in sales. In any given week, he would easily have several paintings out of the door. The phones weren't buzzing as usual. He was frustrated. He even told Casey that she could take the afternoon off as the gallery was so quiet.

The phone screamed. Jack looked at his mobile, happy and yet strangely surprised that the phone had even rung. *Finally*, he said to himself.

'Hello, Jack speaking.'

There was just silence on the other end. Jack waited for the person on the other end to speak.

Still no response.

Then he heard it. A sinister, eerie voice whispered before fading away: *Can you see it?*

'Hello? Hello?'

There was no response after that. Jack heard the line cut off with a click. Jack looked through his phone and realised that it had been a private number.

Jack's eyes found Rossi's painting as the call ended. He wondered what had inspired Rossi to paint such an artwork. Not being an artist himself, he often indulged in asking the artist before the purchase what their inspiration or thoughts had been when they were painting a particular piece. He enjoyed knowing. He often passed their responses on to potential buyers. This had worked well with a lot of his sales; the buyers tended to feel a greater connection with the piece that way.

In this instance, there was no way of knowing. The artist himself had passed away just after finishing it; all Jack knew was that it had been his final work. Stepping in front of it, he scanned the painting, trying to take in all of its finer details. The prominent strokes of black and grey were sure to grab the attention of anyone who looked at it. He moved closer. Then, the same uncanny voice whispered again, just loud enough for him to make out the words, *Can you see it?*

Stunned, Jack tripped over his own feet and fell flat on his back. He was sure that he had heard someone speak directly into his ear. His eyes scoured the gallery franti-cally, but he was alone. He suddenly felt an illogical fear of the painting. He got up on his feet and wondered if it was because his tired mind was over-thinking things. After all, he had been stressing all week about the busi-ness and it was the last day of a week without any sales.

He decided that he should probably call it a day, go back home and rest it off. He looked at the painting a final time before locking the gallery door and leaving for the day, visibly shaken. For the first time, Jack began to feel there was something sinister about the painting.

CHAPTER 5

Jack was unusually silent at the dinner table. He didn't quite know how to tell Amanda what he had experienced earlier that day. He had never encountered something of this nature. He'd certainly never believed in anything of the supernatural world, but the eerie voice in the gallery could not be logically explained. Still, he felt that he should mention something to Amanda. After all, he had always been open with her about everything in his life.

'How was your day at school today?' started Jack.

'You don't wanna know. That kid Philip and some of the other boys in class caused so much trouble. I was glad when class was over. The other teachers tell me that teenage boys will be teenage boys and not to stress too much about it ... and yes, don't forget next week I've got the school trip with the students, and you'll have to manage on your own.' She drifted off for a moment, lost in thought. 'I'm sorry. How was your day?'

'I closed the store not long after lunchtime and came home to rest.'

'Hon, are you okay? It might just be a slow week,' said Amanda, touching him on the shoulder.

'I need to ask you something,' said Jack.

He hesitated for a moment. He wanted reassurance that all that had taken place had simply been a figment of his imagination. He watched as Amanda waited for him to continue. He heaved a sigh of discomfort.

'Jack, you can talk to me. What is it?'

'Something happened at the gallery today. I can't make any sense of it.'

'What happened?'

'Well, I got a phone call from a private number and couldn't quite hear what the person was murmuring on the other side. Then they hung up.'

'Okay, but that could have been a wrong number or something.'

'Yes, it could've been a wrong number but there's more. After the call, I started to analyse Rossi's painting, just trying to figure what he might have been inspired by and what the painting could mean, just in case a buyer happened to be interested—I'd rather provide *some* insight than none at all.'

'What has the phone call got to do with the painting?'

'Well, as I got closer to the painting and looked

through the finer details, especially the white strokes in the middle, I'm very sure I heard a voice say *Can you see it?* The strange call I received—I believe the person murmured that as well ... It was all just ...'

Jack saw that Amanda was processing what he had said. She seemed just as puzzled as he was. Maybe she thought Jack was so stressed from the week that he had mistaken his thoughts for actual voices. From the years he had known her, Jack knew that Amanda was not one to believe in ghost stories.

'Jack, are you sure you were not just tired and hearing things?'

'You're right; I had a very stressful week ... nothing in the gallery is selling. It's okay, love,' said Jack as he leaned in to give her a kiss on the cheek.

Still, Jack was so sure of the voice he had heard in his gallery. It was almost as if the speaker had been right next to him. It was all just odd. As much as it played on his mind, he decided not to bring up the matter any further with Amanda. The same could not be said for his thoughts, which whirred around his mind and could not be put to rest. *Was the painting really so strange that the old man couldn't wait to get rid of it?* He frowned to himself at the idea.

'Jack, it's gonna be okay. Don't spend your Friday night upset. It will be better next week.'

'I'm sorry, just a few things on my mind. You're right ... it could be just this week. It'll be better next week.'

Jack decided not to think about the painting; for now.

CHAPTER 6

An unknown number flashed across Jack's mobile phone as he was about to retire to bed. He wondered who it could be at this time of the night. He certainly didn't want to have a business conversation this late. For a moment, he wondered if he should pick up the phone, then he sighed wearily. The quiet week at the art gallery compelled him to answer—he couldn't afford to miss out on a potential sale. He couldn't see himself waiting till the weekend to respond. If it wasn't for Amanda's insistence that work finish for the weekend once he locked up the gallery on Friday afternoons, Jack would pick up every business call any day of the week.

Jack answered the call, hopeful that it would be an interested buyer. He smiled to himself.

'Jack, speaking.'

'Hi Jack, this is Sergeant Walter from the local police department.'

Jack's smile disappeared rapidly.

'Uh ... yes, Sergeant Walter, how can I help you?'

'I'm afraid I have some bad news.'

'Excuse me?'

'There was a misunderstanding between two men walking near your art gallery. In the feud, one man threw his vodka bottle into your store window along with an ignited cigarette. A fire broke out, and by the time the fire brigade got out there, a lot of your paintings were in flames. The two men who caused the trouble are in custody.'

'What are you saying? Everything in the gallery is gone?'

'Unfortunately, yes. However, we managed to save one of your paintings.'

Jack didn't know how he knew, but he was sure of which painting had survived.

'Could you please hold onto the painting for me and I'll come down to the gallery right away?'

'You can pick up the item at the police station if you want; we will be closing off the area for further police investigation.'

Jack ended the phone call; all his months of hard work had gone up in flames, just like that. He looked at Amanda, who was in complete shock. At last she hugged him, the one thing he needed most. So many things were going wrong and each event seemed to be worse than the last.

CHAPTER 7

The police officers provided Jack with a report of what had happened; however, they couldn't explain a partially exposed dark figure at the bottom of the video footage. There seemed to be someone there, but the street security camera couldn't capture who it was or, indeed, if there was anyone there at all.

'The men reported that they were the only two people at the scene. However, the camera tells us otherwise. There may have been a third person who instigated the fight,' said one of the police officers.

'Well, that's just great! Because of these two or three morons, I no longer have a business!'

'I'm sorry to hear that, sir. Here is the police report that you requested. This is the only piece that survived the fire,' said the police officer as he carefully handed the painting over to Jack.

Jack looked at the painting. He had been right.

Antonio Rossi's last painting was as pristine as the day he bought it. The fire hadn't even got close to it.

He drove home, angry and troubled. Just when he'd thought his art gallery was going to take off, everything was in ashes, except for one painting.

He walked towards his front door. He took a deep breath and gave a sigh of disbelief.

'Hey, how did it go at the police station?' enquired Amanda.

'Well, this is all I have left,' Jack said as he lifted Rossi's painting in front of him with both hands.

Rusty barked violently. Jack raised his eyebrows. Rusty hardly barked at anyone, let alone at Jack.

'Rusty, settle down. What's wrong buddy?' said Amanda, trying to calm him.

'I guess I'm not the only one who's angry.'

'Look, he's not settling down. I'll put him outside so that we can talk,' said Amanda.

Jack sat back on the couch after he had carefully placed the painting in his home art studio. He closed his eyes and pondered his situation. He felt fortunate that he had at least one painting that could be sold at a good price. However, he felt uneasy that he'd been right about which painting had survived.

Suddenly, it dawned upon him. *Why was the old man so eager to get rid of the painting at such a low price?*

He remembered seeing the eviction letter and several overdue bills. Jack couldn't understand why the old man would let such a masterpiece go. He faintly remembered the news surrounding Rossi's death. Rumour had it he had passed away right after he had finished his final piece in an old prison. Jack's good friend Ray had worked as a night security guard at the old prison, yet somehow it had never occurred to him till now to ask Ray about it all.

As Rusty's barking came to an abrupt end, Jack began to feel a twinge of uncertainty about Rossi's painting being in his house.

CHAPTER 8

Jack awoke to a repetitive thudding sound. It sounded as though someone was knocking heavily on his bedroom door or the door next to him. He rolled over to find that Amanda was not in bed with him. He looked at his bedside clock; it was three in the morning.

'Amanda?' he called out.

There was no response. The early morning silence continued to be disturbed by the persistent thudding. He soon realised that the sound was not coming from their room. He got out of bed, looked around and decided to look for Amanda. He opened the bedroom door and the thudding amplified immediately.

'Amanda? Where are you?' he repeated, his voice shaking.

The only reply was another dull thud. The sense of urgency in his voice suddenly increased as he called Amanda's name again. *Where could she be at this time of the night?* Jack thought as he walked towards the hallway. And there she was. Amanda's head was banging against the front door; it seemed like she was trying to run away from something, but again and again she collided with the door. *She must be sleepwalking*, he thought. He rushed to her and gently touched her shoulders.

'Get away from me!' she shouted.

'What? *Amanda!*' exclaimed Jack as she violently pushed him away.

'What am I doing here?' she said as she came to her senses.

'Amanda, are you okay? You must've been sleep-walking,' said Jack as he slowly walked towards her.

Amanda touched her head and looked at Jack in confusion, wondering what she was doing at the front door. Jack rested his hands on her shoulders.

His heart was racing and he was sweating profusely.

'It's okay. Let's get you back to bed.'

'Okay ... I had a really bad dream ...'

'It's okay, Amanda. Let's get back to bed,' he said as he held her hands and walked her back to the bedroom.

Jack's heart was still pumping hard. He did feel intense fear, but seeing how frightened Amanda already was, he didn't want his true emotions to come out. As he closed his eyes, he could not help but wonder what Amanda's bad dream had been about.

CHAPTER 9

Jack found himself lost in thought as breakfast sizzled in the frying pan. He wanted to speak to Amanda about her sleepwalking episode the night before. In the two years that they had lived together, he had never known her to sleepwalk. He was desperate to ask her what had happened.

'Jack ... *Jack!*' said Amanda, trying to get his attention.

'Hey, love. I got up early. I thought we could do with a good meal. Are you okay?' said Jack, noticing that Amanda was holding her head in her hands.

'Yeah, my head feels heavy, that's all. Jack ... there's something I need to tell you.'

'Is it about your sleepwalking?'

'It is more than that. I've never sleepwalked in my life.'

'It's okay, I'm sure it was just a bad—'

'Jack, I had the worst nightmare of my entire life! It's that painting. It's ...'

'It's what?'

'There's something about it ... My nightmare had something to do with it. A dark figure came out of that strange spot in the centre of that painting and it was trying to harm me. I was running away from it. When you touched my shoulder last night, I thought it had got to me. I have no idea how I ended up at our front door.'

'Amanda, I've been meaning to talk to you about something ...'

'What, what is it?'

'Well, I know the painting is strange, but it's just a painting, right? Maybe our minds are just playing games because of all our stress at the moment,' said Jack, attempting to calm his nerves.

'I honestly don't know, Jack. Do you know anything about this painting? Like, why is it so dark and eerie? You've told me that it was painted by a famous artist, but ...'

'Look, I know what you mean ... I'm going to make a few calls today and find out more.'

The painting was untitled, which didn't tell Jack much about its history. He wondered if he should contact the old man from whom he'd bought the painting. After all, the old man would know far more about the artwork than Jack. He also wondered if Ray, who worked at the prison, would know any more about the painting's story.

An urgent knock on the door interrupted Jack's train of thought.

CHAPTER 10

Jack opened the door to two men in police uniforms. They looked concerned. Jack wondered if they were here to discuss the fire at his gallery.

'Are you the owner of this house?' asked one of the police officers.

'Yes, I am.'

'Do you have a pet dog?'

'Yes, Rusty—why do you ask?'

'Sir, someone has alerted the police that there is a deceased dog in your driveway.'

'It wouldn't be my dog, 'cause ... Hang on a sec,' said Jack as he turned away from the officers and rushed towards his backyard.

Rusty was nowhere in sight. Jack rushed back to the door and saw the bloodied dog in his driveway. His heart sank as he walked past the officers to Rusty. In a complete state of shock, he knelt down slowly beside him and burst into tears. Amanda appeared, wondering what all the commotion was about. She saw Jack crouched beside the lifeless Rusty.

'Oh my God, Rusty!' said a grief-stricken Amanda as she rushed towards Jack.

Jack was speechless. The blood that covered Rusty seemed so unreal. *This is not happening*, he thought to himself. The officers waited for Jack to calm down before taking down a statement from him. Amanda, still sobbing, carried Rusty inside the house. The police officers left soon after.

'How could he have got out, Amanda? The gate was locked.'

'I don't—I don't know,' murmured Amanda, through a fresh stream of tears.

Jack rushed to the backyard to investigate. He saw a patch near the side fence that had been dug up; Rusty must have escaped.

Jack examined Rusty's body and it seemed like he had been attacked by another animal. Rusty had four deep claw marks on the side of his body that had caused him to bleed to death.

'He's been attacked by another animal but what kind of animal in this neighbourhood could have managed this? The claw marks are so deep,' said Jack looking bewildered.

'I don't know Jack ... it's just not right ...' Amanda said, sobbing uncontrollably.

'I want to bury him in the backyard,' said Jack as he laid Rusty on a dry towel and wiped away his tears.

'We'll do that for him,' said Amanda, giving Jack a big hug.

Jack buried Rusty and covered him with one final heap of soil.

Afterward, he walked into his home art studio and stared at the painting. He thought of the fire which had consumed his gallery. He thought of Amanda's nightmare. He thought of Rusty's tragic death. With his mind reeling, there was an element in Rusty's death that Jack couldn't put together. The claw marks were so long and deep that only a ferocious animal could have attacked Rusty, not anyone of the pets that he had ever seen in his neighbourhood.

And more still, he couldn't explain the voice he had heard in the gallery. He remembered Rusty's violent reaction to the painting. His thoughts were spinning in tumultuous circles as he sat on his living room couch.

'Jack, I don't think I'll be able to make it for the school trip on Monday. It's a day away and I'm not sure if I'll be able to pull it together,' said Amanda as she sat beside Jack.

Jack watched as Amanda held onto Rusty's collar and began crying again. Tears began to obscure his vision as he pulled Amanda closer to him. He could see that Amanda was drained from all the recent events.

'Love, I think with everything that has happened, a school trip with the kids from school might actually be a good distraction,' said Jack.

'Jack, I don't want to leave you on your own in this state.'

'It's okay. I'll be fine. Just go on the school trip and take your mind off things. I've got something I need to investigate.'

'What do you need to investigate?'

'It's about the painting ... I'm going to give Ray a call.'

Jack wasted no time. He rang Ray at once. They arranged to meet at a quiet cafe first thing on Monday. Jack wasn't sure what he was going to uncover but he was going to go all out to find the answers he was looking for.

CHAPTER 11

Jack sipped his coffee impatiently, waiting for Ray.

'You look really worried, Jack. I'm sorry about the shop and ... Rusty,' said Ray as he sat down beside him at the outdoor cafe.

'Amanda and I will really miss him.'

'How's Amanda holding up with all that's been happening?'

'She's doing her best. She's off on a school trip with her students. She'll be back in a couple of days and hopefully by then I will have found the answers I'm looking for.'

'What is it you want to know?'

'I remember reading in the news that Rossi died in the old prison after he had completed his last painting. Ray, how did he die?'

'Well, he did die in the prison. The media said it was due to natural causes. Look ... you didn't hear it from me, okay? I'm gonna tell you something, but you have to keep it to yourself. Even the news didn't cover this ...'

'What do you mean?'

'Jack, I honestly think, after everything I've heard, the painting is cursed.'

Jack sensed Ray's uneasiness; Ray kept looking around to see if anyone was listening to them.

'I know the full story 'cause there was a senior guard who lost his job—he's a friend of mine, Mario.'

'What has Mario got to do with Antonio's death?'

'Mario let Antonio into the prison after midnight. Antonio wanted to work in the execution chamber to complete the painting; he said he'd only be a couple of hours and would be gone before anyone saw him. No one is allowed into the prison after midnight.'

'So, what happened?'

'Well, Mario got worried when it was past three in the morning and Antonio wasn't picking up his phone, so he went to check on him. He found Antonio on the floor—dead—next to his painting. He called the police and, of course, management eventually found out that he had let someone in after hours and he lost his job.'

'Didn't he die of a heart attack?'

Ray leaned forward. Jack was beginning to feel that the untold story of the painting was about to unfold.

'"Heart attack" is what the report says. I think something happened in that chamber, something that caused him to have a heart attack. It gives me the chills to even think about it.'

'What does Mario think about all this?'

'I don't know, but I'm sure Mario knows more; he might have some more answers. I'll see if he can meet us here,' said Ray, and he began to dial Mario's number.

Jack felt really uncomfortable after his conversation with Ray. He waited restlessly for Mario to meet them at the cafe.

CHAPTER 12

Mario approached the cafe, deep in thought. He was relieved that Ray and Jack had contacted him regarding the painting. He had so much to share with them but none of it was going to be good news. He sat himself down in front of Jack and Ray.

'Mario, thanks for meeting us. I just want to know more about the painting. Ray suggested talking to you,' said Jack.

Mario looked at Jack intensely. He wanted to start from the beginning. He wanted to tell Jack everything he knew about the painting. He wasn't going to miss one detail.

'January, 1964 ... I was eighteen ... I started work at that old prison,' started Mario; then he paused to take a deep breath.

'Mario, we are here to find out about the painting,' urged Ray, slightly confused and glancing at Jack beside him.

'We'll get to that. So … in 1964, there were two convicts due to be executed by hanging that year. It was also the final year in which death row inmates would be hanged in the prison's execution chamber. There was a serial killer they were going to execute at the end of that year and there was another inmate known as the Beast Man who was due to be hanged in a few weeks from the time I joined. The senior guard I was working with wanted me to be one of the guards escorting the Beast Man to the execution chamber on his final day. Our job was to ensure that we woke him up at five in the morning to give him his last meal. Just before eight in the morning, we were to handcuff and walk him to the execution chamber. Once he was in the chamber, we were to put a hood around his head and position him over the trapped door. The lever for the trap door would be pulled at eight in the morning by the executioner who would have a hood on with only his eyes visible,' said Mario.

Mario could sense the impatience of Jack and Ray as he watched them shifting uneasily in their seats. He leaned towards them. He continued to speak once the shifting stopped.

'It was like a furnace in that chamber that time of the year with no ventilation whatsoever in that room. The room smelled stale and of death if you asked me … the executioner, while waiting for the prisoner, took off his hood, which he should never have done. The heat must have got to him, I suppose. No condemned prisoner should ever see their executioner. That's a rule and there's also a belief surrounding it. Unfortunately, the Beast Man saw him and gave him a wicked laugh. The Beast Man then stared deep into the executioner's eyes and kept saying to him, "Can you see it?" … he repeated "Can you see it?" as the executioner frantically began to put on his hood. The Beast Man carried on saying "Can you see it?" as if it were a chant, even as we were about to put his hood on. We asked him if he had any last words. His reply was "Can you see it?" I remember that day vividly. It scares me even till today just thinking or talking about it,' said Mario.

'Mario, I'm really sorry to interrupt you, but what has this Beast Man got to do with the painting?' said Jack looking mystified.

Mario had a deep-seated fear in his eyes. His lips were shaking as he continued.

'The Beast Man has everything to do with that painting. The Beast Man was pure evil. You could see it in his eyes. His pupils were pitch-black and they almost covered his entire eyes. And the reason he got the name Beast Man was because he had these sharp canine teeth similar to that of a vampire. His fingernails were sharp. His fingers were thick and looked like those of a beast.

There were all kinds of convicts in that jail at that time, but this guy emitted a very dark aura all around him. I was told he was in prison for several murders. He had also killed an inmate while he was prison. They had to keep him confined in a cell away from the general prison population while he awaited his execution date. On the day of his execution, the senior guard and I came to his cell to escort him to the chamber. I saw in his cell there were small pieces of charcoal scattered across the ground and the walls were covered in drawings of black circles with blank spaces in the middle. He had also scribbled the words "Can you see it?" everywhere he could.'

'Are you saying there's a link between Antonio's painting and this Beast Man's drawings?' interrupted Jack.

'Yes ... they are strangely similar ... I never told Antonio anything about what I saw in the Beast Man's cell. All I said was it was dangerous to paint in the execution chamber and that there was a date in that prison where no one was allowed in that chamber. It was the date that the Beast Man was executed. I did mention to Antonio that lots of bad things happened on that date when anyone entered it. Antonio wouldn't listen. He wanted to paint and so he did,' said Mario.

Mario paused for a moment. He took a deep breath before he continued speaking.

'By the time I got to the chamber, I found Antonio on the ground with his eyes wide open. I tried to revive him, but he was already dead. His body was stone cold. His left cheek had four claw marks from which blood oozed. Autopsy reports said he had died of a heart attack, but the claw marks remained a mystery ... they could only have been inflicted by an animal's claws, not a human or a sharp object. The whole incident that happened that day at the prison haunts me till today.'

'But Rossi's painting, it's just a painting, right?' said Jack.

'No, it isn't. It killed my best friend. I told Antonio not to paint in that prison, but he wouldn't listen to me. I honestly believe Antonio unleashed some sort of evil which has latched onto this painting. You need to get rid of that painting,' said Mario firmly.

'But don't you think this is all just a coincidence and that the Beast Man being connected to the painting is a little farfetched?'

'Look kid, if you've been listening to anything I've been saying you'll know it's best to get rid of that thing. It's evil. Get rid of it before it's too late! I've got to go ... I've got an appointment with my psychologist. I haven't been able to work since ... since all that.' Mario stood up and left abruptly.

Jack began to process everything Mario had said.

The story of the Beast Man gave him unsettling thoughts. However, the theory that evil could latch onto a painting seemed impossible to him. He just couldn't bring himself to destroy the painting even after all he had heard.

CHAPTER 13

Jack still had his doubts. He wasn't convinced that a painting could be pure evil. Maybe his misfortune was merely a result of the state of his life at that point; a rough patch.

'What should I do with the painting, then? I still haven't heard anything from the insurance company, but I know I can sell the painting at a high price. Things are not going great for me at the moment, Ray.'

'Things are not going great at the moment because of that painting. Like Mario said, that painting is damned. Look, I know someone who knows about these things; I'll give him a call and ask him to meet with us at your place to have a look at Rossi's piece. His name is Toom.'

'What, like some guy who understands spirits and stuff?'

'He's a spiritual guy, yeah—a family friend. And

he seems to know a thing or two about these kinds of situations.'

'I don't know, Ray ... Maybe I should ask the guy I bought the painting from if he knew or felt anything about the painting—'

'Look, Jack, I think you should meet Toom. Let him have a look at the painting and see what he says about it.'

'I don't know if we should go that far.'

'Jack, things have already gone that far. Everything bad that has been happening in your life seems to be because of that painting.'

Jack sighed. 'You might be right. Give Toom a call and ask him to come over and see the painting.'

CHAPTER 14

Jack waited with Ray for Toom to get to his place. The anticipation of what Toom was going to say about the painting was sending his thoughts in circles. Jack sprang out of his couch as soon as there was a knock on the door.

'Hi, I'm Jack. Please come in.'

Toom had wrinkles and lines across his face, indicating a full life. He emitted a sense of calm, with authority. A faded silver cross pendant hung from his neck. Toom hesitated for a brief moment. Jack wondered why.

'Do you have something in your house that you feel uncomfortable about?' started Toom.

'Ray, did you tell him about the painting?' said Jack.

'Toom doesn't know why he's here, other than to talk to you about something, Jack,' Ray replied.

A chill ran down Jack's spine. Toom had barely even entered the house and yet he knew that Jack was uncomfortable about something inside his own home.

'Well, have a seat then, and I'll let you have a look at the painting. Would you like something to drink? Coffee, tea, water?'

'Cold water would be good,' said Toom in a deep voice.

Jack went to the kitchen and took a jug of cold water out of the fridge. He placed two glasses on the counter-top and started to pour water into them. After he had finished drinking his glass of water, he placed his empty glass onto the counter and took Toom's cold glass of water to him.

'So ... can I bring you the painting?' he asked as he watched Toom place his glass of water on the coffee table in front of the couch.

Toom nodded at Jack. Jack could hear whispers of conversation as he walked to his studio to retrieve the painting. He opened the door and took a look at the painting. He wondered what Toom was going to say about it.

Toom stood up from the couch as Jack approached the living room. His eyes grew wide, fixated upon the painting. Ray, sensing that Toom had felt something, stood up as well, as if something was about to happen.

'What is it, Toom?' asked Jack.

'Is this the last painting of Antonio Rossi? The one completed in that old prison?'

'Yes, it is ...' said Jack as he handed the painting over to Toom.

A phone call interrupted the conversation.

'Hi, love, is everything okay?' asked Jack.

'Yes, everything's okay. I'm still feeling down about Rusty and called to see if you were okay,' said Amanda.

'I'm doing okay ... I do miss Rusty, too ... hey, I've actually got Ray and a friend of his over at our place at the moment. It's about the painting,' said Jack.

'Is everything okay?'

'Everything is okay ... I'll tell you more when you get back.'

'Okay, take care of yourself, Jack.'

A glass smashed in the kitchen as the phone call ended.

'What was that?' asked Ray.

'I don't know ... I'll find out,' said Jack as he headed for the kitchen.

Jack went into the kitchen and found a shattered glass on the floor. He realised that the empty glass left on the benchtop had fallen off. He bent over to pick up the pieces.

'Damn it!' exclaimed Jack.

Toom left the painting on the couch and rushed to the kitchen with Ray. Jack was crouched down on the kitchen floor, his left hand covered in blood.

'Jack, are you alright?' asked Ray.

'I shouldn't have tried to get the pieces with my bare hands. It's my fault.'

Ray helped Jack up and brought him to the sink to wash his bloodied hand. Toom looked more serious than before, which only made Jack more fearful of what he was actually dealing with.

Jack sat on the couch, applying pressure to a deep cut on his finger with a bandage. Toom, although unmoved by what had just happened, looked more intense than ever. He had this disturbing calmness about him that Jack couldn't understand.

'You're going to say that this was caused by the painting, aren't you?' said Jack, gesturing to his injured hand.

Toom didn't answer his question. He simply looked wistfully at the dog collar sitting on the living room bookshelf labelled *Rusty*.

'What happened to Rusty?'

'What? Well, he died a few days ago. I think he was attacked by another pet in the neighbourhood,' said Jack, puzzled by Toom's diversion.

'Toom, what is it about the painting you're sensing?' asked Ray, cautiously.

'Have you or your partner been having nightmares or any other form of disturbances?' asked Toom.

'Yes, Amanda has had a nightmare about the painting and the voices ... and yes, I heard a strange voice when I was alone in my gallery before it burnt down,' said Jack.

It suddenly struck Jack. He remembered what Mario had said about the Beast Man chanting "Can you see it?" and his final words. The Beast Man's words were exactly what he had heard in his gallery. Then he recalled the claw marks on the brown paper when he first bought the painting and the claw marks on Rusty. He froze in fear.

'Your partner having nightmares, you hearing a strange voice in your gallery, and your gallery being burnt down all seem to point to one thing ... This painting is cursed. Get rid of it before more terrible things happen,' said Toom as he managed to snap Jack out of a momentary daze.

'More terrible things?' began Jack.

'It will destroy the lives of anyone whose possession it finds itself in. Destroy it—and do it far away from your home,' said Toom sternly.

'Jack, I think Toom is right and we have heard enough of this painting, but the decision is up to you,' insisted Ray.

'Jack, this painting was created in an abhorrent place,' Toom said. 'If I read correctly, the artist died right after he finished this artwork. Don't let it be in your house another day. If it ends up in the hands of someone new, you know what will happen. Get rid of this evil, Jack. I'll help you.'

'Okay. Alright. Wh-what should we do?'

'I need a piece of paper and a pen,' said Toom, abruptly.

Jack hurriedly handed Toom a paper and pen and watched him scribble down the name of a country road.

'Meet me and Ray here once it's dark, about eight at night. We will burn this thing together. I'll get the kerosene and the light; you just go there with the painting,' said Toom definitively.

'Okay,' replied Jack, in agreement.

'And Jack … be careful. I'll see you tonight,' said Toom looking at Jack warily and leaving the house with Ray.

...

Jack was woken up by the sound of thunder. The evening darkness had set in and he realised he had fallen asleep on the couch. As he got up to switch on the lights, he heard the same ghostly voice he had heard in his gallery. *Can you see it?*

Jack shivered and desperately searched for the switch. The voice stopped and his eyes found their way to the painting, which still sat on the couch. It chilled his bones now that he was alone in the darkness staring at it. Another strike of thunder startled him. Then the sound of breaking glasses, one after the other, could be heard from the kitchen. It was as if every single plate and glass he owned was being smashed on the kitchen floor.

Jack looked at his watch. It was thirty minutes to eight. He knew something evil and strange was taking place in his house. He knew it was time to remove this painting from his life once and for all. He shoved his car keys into his pocket, grabbed the painting in one hand and headed for the door. He tried to wrench open his door but could only open it slightly. The wind was howling wildly; it seemed like someone on the outside was preventing him from opening it. He dropped the painting to the ground and using both hands, with all the strength he could muster, he managed to pull the door open. A huge gust of wind thrust him to the ground. He desperately reached for the painting as he gathered the strength to stand up. In partial shock, he finally managed to get out of the house with the painting, locking the door behind him.

The winds continued to roar as a storm began to brew in the distance. He clicked open the garage door. Jack knew for certain that the painting needed to go. He was determined to burn it that very night. All he needed to do was get in the car and drive.

CHAPTER 15

Jack shoved the painting into the back seat of his car. He rushed to the driver's seat and started the engine. The car's radio sounded. He looked into his rear-view mirror. The once prized painting now gave him the creeps. He wanted to burn every bit of it.

He reversed his car out of the driveway. The first drop of rain hit his windscreen with a dull thud. Thunder shook the car, sending vibrations through Jack's body. He felt a tingle in his spine. He looked fiercely into his rear-view mirror again. His fiery stare could have burnt the whole painting there and then. *I'm getting rid of you*, he murmured under his breath. A huge thunderous burst of rain started smashing against the car just as he started to drive. 'Great! But I'm not stopping till you are destroyed and out of my life,' he said out loud.

The windscreen wiper at full blast gave Jack only the slightest visibility. His car seemed to be the only one on the country road on this dark, dreadful night. He began to hear scratching sounds from the back. They started softly and gradually got louder and louder, until he heard the haunting words reverberate throughout the car. *Can you see it?*

He swung around to look at the back seat, for a split second taking his eyes off the road. Time stopped and then a flash of light blinded him. Shattered glass hit his face and he felt a sudden surge of pain. He felt the car jolt into the air, and in that very second the painting hurtled past him, flying straight through the windscreen. It had defeated him. He soon came to realise that the warm sensation across his face was his own blood. As his eyes slowly began to shut, he uttered a weak moan of terror as he spotted the painting, which had come to rest safely at the base of a tree.

CHAPTER 16

Jack opened his eyes. People dressed in black robes filled what appeared to be a strange hall. The hall resembled an old church, yet he felt nothing but evil around him. His body appeared to be paralysed with fear, his ears filled with the heavy pounding of his heart. The faces of the dark figures around him were covered with white ash and their eyes only dark hollows. The leader of their group stepped forward, facing Jack.

'Where am I?'

'You don't need to know where you are. Just walk through that door,' said the leader, menacingly.

Jack turned around and saw an open door at the end of the hall. A bright light shone out of it, so brilliant that he couldn't see what was inside. With a gasp he realised why it felt vaguely familiar. It was the same white light at the centre of Antonio Rossi's painting. Something wasn't right. He knew he was not supposed to be here.

Amidst all this fear and panic, he came to realise that he was dressed in a hospital gown.

He turned back to the leader. 'No, I'm not going through that door. Where am I ... and who are you people?'

The sea of people became angry at his response, and they all began chanting and shouting at him in unison, 'To the door! To the door! To the door!' They walked towards him, a wall of bodies pushing him closer and closer towards the white light.

His cries for help were drowned out. His bloodshot eyes swivelled around once again and looked at the blinding rays of light that burst from the door. As the crowd closed in on him, he came to the painful and fearful realisation that his end was near. His legs started to feel weak; his hands could no longer hold them back.

Then he heard a familiar voice. It was Amanda.

He heard her calling him again. *Jack! Jack! Don't ...*

Her voice was drowned out. The chants became louder. *To the door! To the door! To the door!*

His eyes frantically searched the hall for Amanda but she was nowhere in sight. He knew his end was near; his body felt weak and exhausted from fighting the crowd. Amanda's voice disappeared. He had lost the will and strength to live. His body was just a few steps away from the portal of death.

CHAPTER 17

The painting sat in front of a large crowd of art enthusiasts. One could have examined every inch of it under a microscope and not find a scratch or mark on it. No one would believe that just a few weeks earlier the very same painting had been in a car crash.

The painting stood high on an easel, waiting to be sold to the next soul.

A prized collector's item and the very last work of Antonio Rossi echoed throughout the auction room, bringing the bids even higher. Then the painting caught the attention of a well-dressed man.

The painting had charmed him, encouraging him to raise his bid each and every time another bidder outbid him. The painting had by now formed a strong and unbreakable connection with the gentleman. He was outbidding everyone in the room.

'Sold!' yelled the auctioneer at last.

Within minutes of the auction, a man dressed in a fine suit found himself to be the new owner of the painting. A new horror would soon unfold.

CHAPTER 18

Amanda felt a slight vibration that woke her from her sleep. Jack had finally made his first movement after being in a coma since the car accident. The unfortunate kangaroo he had tried to avoid on the country road had crashed into the side of his car and died instantly. Jack, however, was starting to show signs of life.

'Jack!' Amanda exclaimed.

Amanda couldn't believe it—it was his first movement in four weeks and she was so excited; she wanted to run and get a nurse. Jack's hand grasped her own, as if urging her to stay. His body began to vibrate violently, shaking the bed. Amanda, in a state of shock and excitement, simply froze.

'Nurse!' she shouted, finally managing to find her voice and call for help.

Jack's body started to shake even more violently, as if his soul were about to leave his body.

'Jack! Jack! Don't you die on me! *Nurse!*'

All of a sudden, Jack's body stopped shaking and he settled down. The machine beside him screamed as his heart rate dropped lower and lower. A nurse rushed in to find Amanda in tears.

'Step aside, ma'am,' she said, shouting for the doctor.

Jack's heart had completely stopped beating at this point. The doctor had the nurse prepare the defibrillator.

Amanda saw Jack's body jolt, yet his heart had still not awoken. She could see the desperation of the doctors and nurses as they tried to bring him back to life with a second electric shock. Amanda couldn't believe this was happening. She felt the urge to shout at the doctor, the nurses and Jack. Nothing came out of her mouth. Her throat was tight with pain, desperation and fear.

The third electric shock jolted Jack's lifeless body. It seemed like all was lost. His heart was not responding at all to the powerful voltage that struck it, one jolt after the other, desperately trying to revive it.

The voices in the room began to become muffled as panic and shock hit Amanda. All she could hear were the words *clear, not responding* and *keep trying*.

'All clear!' shouted the nurse.

Jack's body jolted once again without any effect. A surge of emotion spilled over Amanda. She pushed the doctors and nurses aside and grabbed Jack by his shoulders, pulling him towards her.

'Jack! Jack! Wake up!' shouted Amanda.

Everyone froze in time for a brief second as if waiting for a miracle.

CHAPTER 19

The precious moments of waiting for Jack to open his eyes seemed like a lifetime. Amanda prayed that he would snap out of his coma and come back to life.

The machine beside Jack started beeping again, indicating that his heart had been revived.

'Oh my God, Jack!'

'Where am I?' he said in a weak voice, slowly gaining consciousness.

'You're in hospital. You were in an accident and went into a coma.'

'My head ... The painting! Where is it?' said Jack, trying to get out of his bed.

'Jack, calm down. Don't worry about the painting,' said Amanda, preventing him from getting out of bed.

Jack became hysterical. He knew he had to get rid of the painting. He desperately tried to get out of his bed, only to be prevented by the nurses and Amanda.

'I need to get rid of it!' he said with all the strength he had.

'Jack, you don't have to worry about that ...'

A phone call interrupted the commotion. Amanda and Jack watched as Amanda's phone rang. Jack stopped struggling to get out of bed, wondering what news the phone call was going to bring.

'Yes, Amanda here.'

'The painting you had us put on auction was sold just minutes ago,' said the agent.

'Thank you so much, that's great news!' said Amanda, relief in her voice.

Amanda's eye caught Jack. He didn't know what the phone call was about. His head and body were throbbing terribly, but he desperately wanted to get out of bed to destroy the painting, wherever it was.

'It's about the painting, Jack.'

'What about it?' he said, breathing heavily.

'You don't have to worry about it. It was sold just moments ago. I got an agent to sell it off in an auction. I didn't want it in our lives anymore.'

The doctor and nurses left the room.

'Amanda, that painting is evil and I needed to destroy it. It shouldn't be sold to anyone.'

'I didn't know what to do with it, and a friend told me to sell it off at the auction. We needed the money for your medical bills, too. It didn't make sense to destroy it when we needed the money.'

Jack stared blankly ahead of him. He didn't want to think of what would befall the next person who owned the painting. He stretched out his hands to give Amanda a hug, reassuring her that he knew why she did what she did.

'I'm glad that I came back to you.'

'Jack ... I'm so glad you're back. You're alive. Everything's going to be alright now.'

Jack felt pain throughout his body, as if he had been through a battle. The painting was gone. He tried his best not to think about its new owner. He wished he had not even come into possession of it in the first place. He was certain that things were going to be better now that the evil painting was gone from his life.

EPILOGUE

Jack smiled as the last customer left. He felt elated as he looked at his gallery all done up. It was filled with various art pieces and was glowing with life. He felt safe now that the painting was no longer with him. As he closed the till for the day, he called to make reservations at Amanda's favourite restaurant. He was going to give her a treat for all she had done for his recovery and helping him set up his gallery once more.

She had even bought them a new dog, which had cheered him up during his weeks of recovery.

The bad episodes of his life had ended. There were no more terrifying dreams and inexplicable events. The business was thriving and he couldn't have asked for more. As he finished making reservations and hung up, his phone rang almost immediately.

He wondered if he should answer it. He looked at his watch, which told him that it was five minutes to five.

It was a Friday and he certainly didn't want to be late for his date with Amanda. Reluctantly, but promising himself that it would only be a short call, he answered it.

'Hi, am I speaking with Jack?'

'Yes. How can I help you?'

'I'm calling about a painting you used to own.'